10 things I hate about you

A NOVELIZATION BASED ON
THE TOUCHSTONE PICTURES
HIT COMEDY

10 things I hate about you

ADAPTED BY
DAVID LEVITHAN

SCREENPLAY WRITTEN BY
KAREN McCULLAH LUTZ & KIRSTEN SMITH

BASED ON
"THE TAMING OF THE SHREW" BY WILLIAM SHAKESPEARE

SCHOLASTIC INC.
New York Toronto London Auckland Sydney
Mexico City New Delhi Hong Kong

ISBN 0-439-08730-9

12 11 10 9 8 7 6 5 4 3 2 1   9/9 0 1 2 3 4/0

Printed in the U.S.A.

First printing, April 1999

For Eliza
may we always end up in the same place

1
Kat

I am a prisoner. Padua High School is my prison. From seven forty-five every morning to two twenty-five every afternoon (with the exception of weekends, mental health days, air breaks, and study hall walkouts), I am sentenced to a mind-numbing barrage of senseless information, surrounded by senseless student Drones. Like every prisoner, I must have a strategy for survival. If I let my guard down, the airheaded masses might suck me into their wannabe popularity whirl. I must defend myself. And sometimes the best defense is to *be* offensive.

Perky girls roam the hallways like unhinged talk show hostesses. Steroid-brained guys flex self-satisfied smiles and think no more than two times a week. They have less attractive underlings to do their homework for them, smart kids who aren't smart enough to realize they're fools.

My youngest sister, Bianca, is the Queen of the Drones. She's a sophomore, but she acts like she's in kindergarten. Boys fall over their feet whenever she's around. She's used to it by now. She doesn't mind being in a prison, as long as her uniform is from J. Crew.

I have no desire to be a Drone. I hold my head high and my eyes open. They're not going to get to me.

I am their Anti-Prom Witch Nightmare Girl.

They understand me even less than I understand them.

2
Cameron

Another new school. After a while, they all start to seem the same. This time, Dad promised me we would stay until I graduated. He said Padua High School could give me the best education in America. Far better than the Pisa, New Jersey, school system I'm coming from. But if it's such an exceptional place, why does it look like everywhere else?

A guy named Michael shows me around. At first, I think he's an exception to the rule — usually, the new boy gets matched up with an audiovisual geek. Michael seems different . . . until some guy with a video cart comes over and asks him where to put his slides. Oh, well.

At least Michael seems to have a grasp of the Padua social situation. This is important for every new kid to understand. In Pisa, there were the Patio People (smoke central), the Charlie Roses (Yale-to-be's), the Mallflowers (also known as the Platinum Cards), and the Leaning Towers (don't ask).

"So, Cameron," Michael says, guiding me around the hallways, "here's the breakdown. Over there we've got your basic Beautiful People. Unless they talk to you first, don't bother."

I wonder aloud whether this is their rule or Michael's. Michael doesn't answer but instead gets blown off by a Beautiful Person, to prove his point.

Next we pass an espresso cart. It must be a Seattle thing.

"To the left, we have the Coffee Kids," Michael explains. A brawl starts because someone has spilled some Costa Rican beanage.

"Very edgy," Michael warns me. "Don't make any sudden movements around them." Next he points out a posse of Skaburbanites.

"These delusionals are the White Rastas. Big Marley fans. Think they're black."

4

They seem to be a little better than the White Ghetto Boyz in Pisa.

Then there are the White White Guys. Stetson-wearing, big-belt-buckle, Wrangler guys.

"Let me guess," I say. "The Cowboys?" (This can't possibly be a Seattle thing.)

"Yeah," Michael confirms, "but the closest they've been to a cow is McDonald's."

Finally, we hit the Future MBAs. (FYI, MBA = Moneyed, Boring, and Arrogant.)

"Yesterday," Michael says with a sigh, "I was their god."

I ask him what happened. He tells me Bogey, their leader, started a rumor that he bought his Izods at an outlet mall.

"And they kicked you out?" I ask.

"Hostile takeover," Michael replies. "But don't worry, he'll pay."

I hear my dad's words again — this is my home until I graduate. I have to admit, I start to get scared. There doesn't seem to be anything to make me want to stay.

And then I see her.

Pure and perfect, gliding through the halls.

It's as if the whole world has stopped,

and there is only her. She is the only thing I can see.

A secret smile. A dream.

I burn, I pine, I perish.

Michael teases me. When I ask, he says she's from the "don't think about it" group. He says she has an incredibly uptight father, and that she's not allowed to date.

But I don't want to date her. I want to marry her.

Nothing that Michael says matters, except for her name: Bianca Stratford.

Bianca.

3
Kat

The prison is run by idiots. They are an insult to the word *teacher*. Teachers are wonderful beings who inspire the spirit and open the mind.

Nobody at Padua High School fits that description.

Take Mr. Morgan, my lit-er-a-*ture* teacher. He wheels out the regular Dead White Guys — like we haven't heard *that* deal before. If you dare to disagree with him, he sends you to the guidance counselor. Now *that's* an education.

And if the Dead White Guys aren't bad enough, I also have to contend with the Living White Guys who sit around me in Mr. Morgan's class. I mean, Hemingway was an abusive, alcoholic, misogynistic jerk, but at least he could write well. Joey Donner, on the other hand, is an abusive, alcoholic, misogynistic jerk who has a hard time spelling ESPN. He is constantly on my case because he can't stand the fact that I have a mind of my own and don't think he's a Super Duper Football Hustler God.

I can see right through him.

You can tell from his snide remarks and his "It must be that time of the month" jokes that I scare him.

Good.

Sometimes I spend Mr. Morgan's class plotting gruesome ways for Joey to die. (No all-female jury would ever convict me.) Other times I pretend to be reading a Dead White Guy when I'm really reading a Young Female Anarchist.

Today I don't really have a chance to do either, since Mr. Morgan kicks me out of class after five minutes. Nowhere close to my one-point-three-second record. But still.

I'm sent down once again to Ms. Perky's office (that's her real name, swear to Goddess). The temptation to bolt is high, but if I bolt, I will be stuck in prison for extra hours. And that is *not* desirable.

Ms. Perky wants you to think she's got an iron will, but really she's got a heart of Danielle Steel. During school hours, she works on her romance novel. (If romance isn't already dead, then Ms. Perky is definitely going to kill it. Good riddance, I say. Maybe if she kills it, people will start to act a little more sane.)

Ms. Perky and I have a routine for situations like this — at this point, it's well rehearsed, and today it plays out predictably.

"So I hear you were terrorizing Mr. Morgan's class again?" she says.

"Expressing my opinion is not a terrorist action," I reply. Although it's clear that *some* prison officials think it is.

Of course, Ms. Perky brings up my past "misdeeds" (like the whole Bobby Ridgeway incident, although I still maintain that he kicked himself). Then I am blessed with Ms. Perky's assessment of my character — that I'm tempestuous, evil, unlikable, etc. As if she conducted a guidance counselor poll, and I scored lower than a puppy killer.

"You might want to work on that," Ms. Perky says sweetly.

"As always, thank you for your excellent guidance," I reply even more sweetly.

We both want a death match so badly that I can almost taste the blood.

After school, I commiserate with Mandella. She's the only person at Padua High School I can talk to. She's kind and considerate — I don't know how she can survive. It helps that she is totally infatuated with William Shakespeare, the ultimate Dead White Guy. If you're strange enough, people won't notice you're kind and will leave you alone.

Of course, Mandella is aghast at the whole Ms. Perky situation. But she is even more shocked by Bianca's English class, which she was assisting. Apparently, no one read the assignment. And the assignment was written by *Mandella's* DWG.

"Your sister is so amazingly *without*," Mandella informs me (ooh — alert the media!). "She's never even read William. She'll never understand . . ."

Of course, not everyone can be in love with a DWG. But at least Mandella feels she's qualified. She copies down ten sonnets every night before she goes to sleep. And she and some other Shakespeare freaks have this chat room on weekends, where they each take roles and then type out their characters' lines to "act out" one of the Bardy Boy's plays.

All in all, it's pretty tame, as obsessions go. I'm just glad my only friend isn't addicted to something really toxic, like the Backsync Five (or whatever they're called). I'd have to deprogram her if she were.

Sometimes it's strange when Mandella takes some time off from Willie World and comes back to Earth. Like now. I'm trying to sneak a glance at our resident long-haired, cell block D, yum guy, and she catches me.

"Who's that?" she asks.

"Patrick Verona. Random skid."

"*That's* Patrick Verona?" she gasps. (Clearly, you can't learn subtlety from Shakespeare.) "The one who was gone for a year?"

Everybody wonders why he disappeared.

I wonder why he came back.

4

Cameron

I have competition.

The worst kind of competition.

In my mind, there are two kinds of looking. There's the kind of looking that is respectful, almost magical, where you observe something without daring to touch it. And then there's the kind of looking that's like slurping a Coke.

He is looking at Bianca like he's thirsty. Like he wants to claim and devour her.

"Who's that guy?" I ask Michael.

"Joey Donner. He's a jerk. And a model. Mostly regional stuff, but he's rumored to have a big tube sock ad coming out."

Do I really have to be like him in order to get this girl?

Whatever it takes, I'll do it. Whoever I must become, I'll become.

Sacred and sweet is all I see in Bianca.

"Look at her," I say. "Is she always so —"

"Vapid?" Michael interrupts.

"How can you say that?" I can't believe it. "She's —"

"Conceited?"

"C'mon," I say, "there's more to her than you think. Look at her eyes, her smile. She's completely pure. I'm telling you you're missing what's really there."

Michael is not convinced. Clearly he has some issues. "What's there is a snotty little princess," he tells me, "wearing a strategically placed sundress to make guys like us realize we can never touch her, and guys like Joey realize they want to. She, my friend, is what we will spend the rest of our lives not having."

I tell Michael he's wrong about her.

"You wanna take your shot," he says, "be my guest. She's looking for a French tutor."

"Perfect!"

"You speak French?"

13

"No . . . but I will."

I would be a slave to achieve the maid whose sudden sight has thrilled my wounded eye.

French is the least I can do.

5
Bianca

Joey Donner said hi to me in the hall!

Oh! My! God!

It was right before English class. And I know I could be making something out of nothing, but the way I see it, Joey Donner doesn't have to say hi to anyone he doesn't want to say hi to, so if he said hi to me in the hall, it probably means that he meant to say hi to me, which absolutely means he knows that I exist, which is the best news I have ever heard in my whole life.

Chastity is SO HAPPY for me, and I am SO HAPPY to have a best friend like Chastity.

It's, like, how this morning she and I were talking about like and love. I don't know which one I feel about Joey.

"There's a difference between like and love," I told her. "I *like* my Skechers. But I *love* my Prada backpack."

"But I love my Skechers," Chastity argued.

I thought about that a second and then I said, "That's because you don't have a Prada backpack."

And she said, "Oh."

We're like that. We can talk about anything. Deep things, too.

So I am telling Chastity all about Joey after school for, like, the seventeen-thousandth time. And then I hear this revving noise.

Is it the sound of my heart?

No — it's the sound of Joey's car!

"Would you sweet young things like a ride?" he says with this twinkle in his *amazing* eyes.

I can't get into the car fast enough.

It's like being ready to pay full price for a top and then learning it's on sale.

No — it's like being ready to pay full price for a top and then learning it's free!

"Careful on the leather, now," Joey goes.

He's *so* considerate. Even about his car.

I can barely speak as we pull away.

You know how they say that time flies when you're having fun? Well, what they don't tell you is that time REALLY flies when you're with a hot guy that you kind of like. We drive around for a while, and Chastity chats, and I can't find the words, and Joey doesn't say much, either, and that's okay, because Joey isn't the kind of person who will say something unless he really, really means it. I don't know how I know this about him. I just do. Sometimes our eyes meet when he looks in the rearview mirror. And that says more than anything else.

Before I know it, we're pulling up in front of my house, and Chastity is saying good-bye, and Joey is nodding at me, and I'm feeling all sad until I realize . . .

I didn't have to tell Joey where I lived.

HE ALREADY KNEW WHERE I LIVED!

This is a definite development.

I have to stop a second before I open the door to the house. Because I am BEAMING and I can't see Daddy quite yet, because if he takes one look at me he'll know what's going on, and then I'll receive this week's lecture of the century. I love Daddy to death, and I know he wants me to be happy. But his

17

idea of happy and my idea of happy are two very different ideas of happy, so it's best if I only show his kind of happy when he's around. It works for us all that way.

Of course, the High Priestess of Doom and Gloom is also waiting for me when I walk in. I never have to worry that my older sister, Kat, will show the wrong kind of happy. She doesn't seem to know that happy even exists.

No — her mental stereo plays only pain pain pain, and it's set on repeat.

Before I walk in, I hear Daddy say, "Hello, Katarina. Make anyone cry today?"

"Sadly, no," she says back. "But it's only four-thirty."

Ha ha.

I put Daddy in a better mood. "Hello, precious," he says, and I love that. Ever since Mommy left, Daddy has had a very hard time. But when he calls me "precious," it's like it's his way of saying everything is going to be okay.

He's brought in the mail. I can see there aren't any catalogs, so I'm not particularly interested. Then Daddy says that someone named Sarah Lawrence wrote to Kat, and she

freaks out. I swear to God, she even looks —
is it, like, even possible? — excited. I wonder if she is so starved for human contact
that a random letter from a long-distance
pen pal could make her so un-Kat.

Then she says, "I got in!" and I realize
that Sarah Lawrence isn't a *person*. It's a
place. Like Eddie Bauer.

"But Sarah Lawrence is on the other
side of the country," Daddy sputters.

Kat shoots him a *duh* look and says,
"Thus the basis of its appeal."

Daddy looks sad. "I thought we decided
you were going to school here," he says to
Kat. "At U Dub. You know, be a Husky."

"No, YOU decided," Kat barks back. All
traces of humanity are gone from her face.

"So you're just going to pack up and
leave?" Daddy's all anxious now. His voice
is so lost that I want to give him a hug. But
Kat doesn't notice. She is so mean. I say I
HOPE she's going to pack up and leave.

Which of course sets her off.

"Ask Bianca who drove her home," she
snarls.

I want to die. No — first I want to kill her.
Then I want to die.

I try damage control.

"Now don't get upset, Daddy," I say in my cutest, calmest voice. "But there's this boy —"

"— who's a flaming imbecile," Kat interrupts.

I will not let her derail me. "And I think he might ask —"

But of course I don't get to finish my sentence. I never get to finish that particular sentence.

You know how car alarms have panic buttons? Well, Daddy has a panic button like that. With cars, you press the button and the alarm goes off and the car won't start for, like, five minutes. With Daddy, all you have to say is the word *boy*, and his alarm goes off and he won't listen to anything you have to say for the rest of the night.

"Please!" Daddy says. "I know what he's going to ask. And I know the answer: No! The house rule specifically states: No dating until you graduate. End of discussion."

As if he has to remind me what the house rule states. As if there's even a discussion to end.

"Daddy, that's so unfair!" I cry. I know it's pointless, but I always find myself arguing anyway. As if anything short of a miracle would ever make Daddy change his mind. Besides the fact that Mommy left to be with someone else, the fact that Daddy is a doctor and spends his days delivering babies to teenage moms makes him a little tense when it comes to girl-guy things.

"I delivered a set of twins to a fifteen-year-old this morning," he bellows. "You know what she said to me? She said, 'I should've listened to my father.'"

"Yeah, right," I say.

"Well," Daddy protests, "that's what she would've said if she hadn't been so doped up."

"Um, can we focus on *me* for a second?" I ask. "I'm the only girl in school who's not dating."

"No you're not," he points out. "Your sister doesn't date."

"And I don't intend to," Kat adds, just to annoy me. Like she's PROUD of it.

This is, of course, exactly what my father wants to hear. Which I don't think is fair because Kat hardly counts as a girl, and really what she does has nothing to do with my life.

I'm about to tune out on the whole conversation (face it, I've heard it before).

Then Daddy says the three strangest, most amazing words in the English language: "Bianca, you're right."

I haven't even said anything! I want to jump for joy, and call Chastity and Kirsten and Kristin and all of my other friends.

"We throw out the old rule," Daddy says.

If only he stopped there!

Because then he's, like, "New rule — you can date when she does."

It's like I've landed in the most perfect place in the universe. And then it blows up.

I can't date until Kat does.

Which is never.

Never ever.

Never never ever.

"But she's a mutant!" I cry. "What if she never dates?"

"Then neither will you," Daddy says. "And I'll get to sleep at night."

TAKE SLEEPING PILLS LIKE THE REST OF MY FRIENDS' PARENTS! I want to yell. But I don't. Yelling will only make it worse. If that's possible.

Daddy's beeper goes off, and he's gone before I can get myself together.

This is the worst possible news.

Kat is, like, glowing.

She can ruin her own life, but why does she have to ruin mine?

"Can't you find some loser to take you to the movies so I can have at least one date?" I scream. As soon as I say it I'm even more angry because once again Kat has made me stoop to her level of talking.

"Sorry," she says. "Looks like you'll have to miss out on the witty repartee of Joey Donner." Like she can't be happier. Any thought she might have ever had of dating is now gone.

She hates me that much.

And I don't know if I'm strong enough to hate her back.

6
Cameron

A week later, I wait for Bianca in the tutoring room. I have spent the whole night and the whole morning reading French. I have eaten French Toast, and French Fries dipped in French Dressing, just for inspiration.

As if I need further inspiration!

She arrives, and my heart lurches. Then I feel a shiver. Her fair features are shadowed by sadness. Or maybe it's just distraction. Everything has worked out so perfectly so far — the tutoring supervisor spoke only in English when he signed me up to tutor French. Now Bianca comes right to my table. But it feels like I've already lost her.

"Hi!" she says. (My heart lifts.) "Can we

make this quick?" she adds. (My heart falls.) "Roxanne Korrine and Andrew Jaret are having an incredibly horrendous public breakup on the quad. Again."

Courage. I need courage. Because this is surely the stupidest idea in the history of guys liking girls.

"I thought we'd start with pronunciation, if that's okay with you," I say. I nearly choke on the word *pronunciation.*

"Not the hacking and gagging and spitting part. Please." (She has such a unique way of seeing things!)

Courage.

"Well," I say. "There's an alternative."

"There is?" she asks.

"French food. We could, like, maybe eat some. Saturday night?"

Two seconds pass. I have made the biggest mistake of my life.

"You're asking me out," she says. (She noticed!) "That's so cute." (I'm cute!) "What's your name again?" (Thud. The sound of my heart hitting the linoleum.)

I remind her I'm Cameron and let her know that I know about her father's dating rule. I've come up with a way to get past it.

If she tells him she's going on a French class field trip, how could he say no?

"Wait a minute, Curtis," she says. (For her, I'd change my name to Curtis.) "My father just came up with a new rule — that I can date when my sister does."

"You're kidding!" I tell her. This is too easy! "Do you like sailing, because I read about this place that rents boats and —"

"*Beaucoup problemo,* Calvin," she interrupts. (I don't mind! I don't even point out she's mixing languages.) "In case you haven't heard, my sister's a particularly hideous breed of loser."

"Yeah," I say. "I've noticed she's a little . . . antisocial. Why is that?"

"Unsolved mystery," Bianca says with the most beautiful sigh. "She used to be really popular and then it's just like she got sick of it or something. Theories abound as to why, but I am pretty sure she's incapable of human interaction."

There has to be hope! I tell her I'm sure there are lots of guys who wouldn't mind going out with someone difficult. I mean, people bail out of airplanes and board off cliffs. It would be like Extreme Dating.

"You think you can find someone *that* extreme?" she asks innocently.

"Why not?" I say. I can only think of reasons why.

"And you'd do that? For me?"

I can tell she's with me now. She's really seeing me as someone who can do things. Someone she could like.

I tell her I will see what I can do.

I play it real cool.

But inside, I'm burning.

7
Michael

Cameron doesn't get it. I mean, he just doesn't get it.

There are rules.

You cannot take up two spaces in the high school parking lot unless you are popular and driving a sports utility vehicle. Or unless you're Kat Stratford and do it just to be obnoxious.

You cannot wear the same sweater as Joey Donner on the same day that he wears it. If you do, you must immediately change into your gym shirt for the rest of the day.

You cannot sit at a popular cafeteria table unless explicitly invited to do so.

And you cannot, under any circumstances, ask out the most beautiful girl in the school.

"You're in school for one day and you ask out the most beautiful girl?" I yell at Cameron. "Have you no concept of the high school social code?"

"She said yes," Cameron says.

Well, pick me up off the floor.

"She actually *said* she would go out with you?" I cannot believe my ears.

"Yeah. Well, me, Curtis, or Calvin."

"Curtis or Calvin?" I ask.

"Trust me," Cameron says. "Those guys don't stand a chance."

I tell him that if he goes out with Bianca, he'll be set. He'll outrank everyone. Strictly A-list.

With me by his side.

"I thought you hated those people," Cameron says. (He really doesn't get it.)

"Yeah," I reply, "but that was before I knew I had a shot at being one."

Of course, there's a hitch to the whole thing. A mighty big one.

We have to find a date for Bianca's shrew sister.

The mewling rampalian wretch herself.

The rules are never broken easily.

8

Cameron

I am doomed.

9
Michael

So we try asking just about every guy at PHS. We try the Advanced Placements and the Cowboys. We try the Mentos and the Militants. We do not discriminate. And what we find is this:

No matter who they are, no matter how desperate they've become, not a single XY will consider even *considering* a date with Kat Stratford.

And that's putting it politely.

Cameron looks like he's going to get all last-act Romeo on me. He even gets it into his head to approach Patrick Verona, our resident criminal element. I mean, I heard he just did a year in San Quentin for lighting a state trooper on fire. And before that, he sold his own liver on the black market for a new set of speakers.

I know girls always go for the wrong guys, but we're talking serious *Springer* territory here.

Still, Cameron is determined. He sees the guy pulling a Benihana on an innocent embalmed science-lab frog and says he's found his man.

Then, in woodshop, he makes his approach. (This is *without me around*, I might add. The boy should never try to strike out on his own.) Patrick doesn't say one word to him. He just drills a hole in Cameron's French book.

Real classy.

But Cameron still thinks Patrick's the one for Kat. Maybe he thinks the two deviants will get along like old pals.

Maybe he's right.

The problem is: We don't have any money to pay him for the job.

What we need, I realize, is a backer. Someone with money who's stupid.

In a word: Joey Donner.

Before Cameron can react, I make my

move. I figure it's best to leave him out of the more serious negotiations. You see, I've developed what I'd like to think of as a personal style. And Cameron would just botch it up.

So I head, real confident, to Joey's cafeteria table.

I am in total control of the situation.

This is how it goes:

Joey: "Are you lost?" (Clearly, he feels the need to put me in my place.)

Me: "Nope — just came by to chat." (Hah! Put him in *his* place.)

Joey: "We don't chat."

Me (real cool): "Well, actually, I thought I'd run an idea by you. Just to see if you're interested."

Joey: "I'm not."

He grabs me and draws something on my face with Magic Marker. But I'm not going to let him throw me off balance. You see, I've seen *The Godfather* at least twenty times, and I know how to negotiate. Never let them see you sweat.

Me: "Hear me out. You want Bianca, right?"

Joey pretends to ignore me, probably for the benefit of his hulking, thought-challenged friends. But I've got him. I know it.

Me: "But she can't go out with you because her sister is this insane head case and no one will go out with *her,* right?"

Joey: "Does this conversation have a purpose?"

Me (going in for the kill!): "What you need to do is hire a guy who'll go out with Kat. Someone who doesn't scare easily."

I point to Patrick, slacking by.

Joey: "That guy? I heard he ate a live duck once."

Me (even though this is one I haven't heard before): "Everything but the beak and the feet. Clearly, he's a solid investment."

Joey (looking at me now like an equal): "What's in it for you?"

Me (total Al Pacino casual): "Hey, I'm walking down the hall, I say hello to you, you say hello to me."

Joey: "Yeah, I get it. You're cool by association. I'll think about it."

Yes!

Cameron, of course, does not understand the *complexity* and the *subtlety* of what I've done. But I explain it to him: We let Joey pretend he's calling the shots, and while he's busy setting up the shots, Cameron has time with Bianca.

I am a genius.

Albeit, as Cameron confirms, one with an obscene drawing on his face.

10
Kat

I am in absolutely no mood to listen to Mandella moon over Shakespeare. All I can think of is my father saying "U Dub U Dub" — the University of Washington, my next prison sentence. To make matters worse, today I overheard a totally roasted pair of Coffee Girls in the girls' room, while I was stalling. This is what they said:

Coffee Girl A: "I've got a quiz in Mr. Morgan's next period. Hit me with the bean."

Coffee Girl B: "Isn't Kat Stratford in that class? What is *up* with her? Mad cow disease?"

CG A: "I heard she ran over some guy in the parking lot last week, and he's, like, dead now."

Then my darling sister chimed in.

"Who told you that?" she demanded.

Coffee Girl A began to apologize to her. I took that as a cue and stepped out of the stall.

"Don't apologize to her," I growled (really, it's too easy). "Apologize to me . . . before I kill again."

I took the cigarette from CG B's hand and dunked it in her java. As I headed out the door, Bianca called, "Did you kill someone and not tell me?"

Yes, sweetheart. Blew up the Delia's warehouse, too.

Goddess help me.

Mandella is not happy when I rag on her Bard-throb. I immediately apologize and explain to her that my dad is insisting that I go to his male-dominated, puking frat boy school. So I can be, of all things, a Husky.

Mandella says my father is acting this way because of the whole Mom situation, and because he doesn't want to let his daughters out of his sight.

I point out that if I were Bianca, it would be, "Any school you want, precious. Don't forget your tiara."

Mandella notes, "You had your chance to be Bianca." Ouch! She must be annoyed 'cuz I'm not in a Bardy-going mood.

"Popularity is overrated," I insist. "If I ever act like Bianca, shoot me."

Through my fake bubblegum heart.

At this point, Mystery Man walks by. Mandella tells me that Candace Parker (*idiot alert!*) told her he was a roadie for Marilyn Manson. And that his so-fake Australian accent comes from when he was forced to live among Pygmies.

Of course.

So obvious.

I wonder: If people stopped gossiping, what would they do with all the extra time? Would they actually get a life? Or would they simply start murdering people in a more obvious way?

Sometimes the best revenge is to act out your reputation.

If you have no other choice.

11

Cameron

French is the language of love. Why else would anyone study it? It's not as if anyone in the world really speaks it anymore.

"C'est ma tête," Bianca says to me.

Then she translates: "This is my head."

French makes everything sound beautiful . . . just like Bianca. We sit side by side now at the tutoring table. My leg barely — just barely — touches her leg.

The plan is working, even if it hasn't really started yet.

"I've never in my life had to point out my head to someone," she observes.

"In Paris," I joke, "it's common courtesy. 'Good morning. How are you? This is my head.'"

It's everything to me to see that glimmer of a laugh cross her face.

"Forget French," she says, closing my book. She hasn't even noticed the hole that Patrick drilled into it. "How is our little find-the-wench-a-man plan progressing?"

I tell her I've found someone.

"Is he demented?" she asks.

I say yes.

"Deranged?"

You bet.

"Chemically imbalanced."

Well, I'm no doctor, but . . .

"He sounds perfect," she says.

God, I hope he is.

12
Patrick

I have these thoughts. I imagine I'm the only person in the whole world. I can move around without having to see a single other person. I can do what I want to do. Nobody stands in my way. Nobody can touch me. I can be as quiet as I want. I can be as loud as I want. Nobody cares.

My life is my own.

And then these thoughts end. I crash back to Earth. This time I come back and see some guy walking toward me. I'm in the bleachers with Scurvy. This guy (Joey?) comes up and starts talking to me.

"Do I know you?" I ask.

"See that girl?" he says, pointing to this fierce soccer girl.

"Yeah." I see her.

"I want you to go out with her."

"Sure, Sparky," I say.

He tells me he can't take her sister out until she starts dating.

Like I care.

"That's a touching story," I tell him. "Not my problem."

"Would you be willing to make it your problem if I provide generous compensation?"

"You're going to *pay* me to take out some girl?" (And they think *I'm* strange.) "How much?"

"Twenty bucks."

I look over and see this girl pounding the other players like they're the ball.

The guy follows my glance and says, "Fine. Thirty."

This is easy money. I can tell I've got him hooked.

"Let's think about this," I think aloud. "Say I take her to the movies — that's fifteen bucks. We get popcorn, it's up to fifty-three. She wants Raisinets, we're looking at seventy-five."

"This isn't a negotiation. Take it or leave it, Trailer Park."

"Fifty bucks and we've got a deal, Fabio."

He pulls out his wallet. It's settled.

I figure I might as well start right away. I make my move to where she is. When she comes off the field, I'm ready.

It doesn't really matter who she is. It's money. Nothing personal.

"Hey, girlie," I say. "How ya doin'?"

I make the most of my accent. Girls *love* the accent.

"Sweating like a pig, actually." She kicks it back to me with this big, wide, you're-a-jerk grin. "And yourself?"

"There's a way to get a guy's attention," I tell her.

"My mission in life. Obviously I've struck *your* fancy. So, you see, it worked. The world makes sense again."

"Pick you up Friday, then," I say.

"Oh, right," she groans. "Friday. Hmmm."

I step closer.

"The night I take you to places you've never been before."

"Really, like where? The 7-Eleven on Broadway? Do you even know my name?"

"I know a lot more than that."

"Doubtful," she says. "Very doubtful."

Then she runs off.

And I'm one step forward.

I'll have to play this just right.

13
Kat

I don't understand it. If they can make bug repellent, why can't they invent boy repellent? After all, bugs are much more intelligent.

I'm thinking this as I wash my face before bed, trying to scrub off all the dirty looks and bad feelings and boy exhalations that I've had to endure during the day. All of the Drone nonsense and empty flirting. All of the gossip and innuendo.

I want it all to be gone, so it won't follow me to sleep.

I am close to clean when Bianca walks in.

Right away, she's after me.

"Have you *ever* considered a new look?" she asks. "I mean, seriously, you have some

definite potential buried under all this hostil-
ity."

That's her idea of a compliment. Which is almost acceptable, except for the fact that it's an insult.

"I'm not hostile," I explain. "I'm annoyed."

"Why don't you try being nice?" she continues. "People wouldn't know what to think."

"You forget," I say. "I don't care what people think."

"Yes you do," she replies.

She really believes this. And the reason she does is because she can't conceive that there's any other way to live her life. I can kind of sympathize with that. I used to make the same mistake.

"No I don't," I tell her gently. "You don't always have to be who they want you to be, you know."

Don't lock yourself in their prison. . . .

"I happen to like being adored, thank you," Bianca responds.

I give up. She's too far gone.

I'm about to say something to this effect when I see the strand of pearls around her neck. I ask her where she got them, and she tells me they're Mom's.

I can't believe it. I ask her if she's been hiding them for the past three years, since Mom left. And she says no — Dad gave them to her.

Just like that.

Mom's pearls.

I don't know why it gets to me, but it does. There are just some moments when life seems so monumentally unfair that I just want to scream and rage and cry and fall apart.

This is one of those times. I'm on the verge.

"So you're just going to start wearing them now?" I demand.

Defensively, she says, "It's not like she's coming back to claim them. Besides, they look good on me."

"Trust me," I snark, barely getting out the words, "they don't."

I have to leave the room. I have to leave Bianca and her false, false world.

I have to leave them, because there are so many other things I cannot leave.

Like my thoughts.

Like my life.

14
Patrick

Day two. Me and Kat. (That's her name.)

Straightforward hallway encounter.

I cue up "Good Lovin'" in my mind and get to work.

"Hey," I say. Big smile. Casual tone.

She doesn't answer.

Perfect.

"You hate me, don't you?" I challenge.

She looks up at me and I'm surprised for a moment because she has pretty cool eyes.

"I don't really think you warrant that strong an emotion."

"Then say you'll spend Dollar Night at the track with me," I plow ahead. It doesn't really matter what she says as long as I get to say the right things.

"And why would I do that?" she asks, naturally.

"Come on," I say. "The ponies, the flat beer, me with my arm around you . . ."

"You, covered in my vomit."

She slams the locker — intense — and walks away.

"Seven-thirty, then?" I call out, undeterred.

It doesn't matter if she hears me.

Although it would be better if she did.

15
Kat

As if my life wasn't bad enough, I now have my own personal stalker.

I don't care what he looks like.

I want him to go away.

Like this afternoon. I find the new Ani CD at the local music store, and I can't wait to get home and soak up her music and her words. But, obstacle: As soon as I get out to my car, I find Stalker Man sitting on the hood, smoking his ever-present cancer stick.

"Nice ride," he says. Like he's Fonzie cool. "Vintage fenders."

Whatever. I accuse him of following me. He claims he was in the laundromat, saw my car, and thought he'd say hi.

The laundromat? Give me a break.

I give him my biggest fake hi and get in the car.

"Not a big talker, huh?" he continues.

"Depends on the topic," I say. "My *fenders* don't exactly whip me into a verbal frenzy."

"You're not afraid of me, are you?"

What is this, a game of double dare? Are we six years old again?

Enough. I grab him by the collar and pull him close. He smells of sweat and woodwork and a hint of cologne.

Nice touch.

"Why would I be afraid of you?" I growl.

"Most people are," he replies.

"I'm not," I assure him. Then I let go and put the car in reverse.

"Admit it," he goes on. "You've thought about me. A lot."

Bad move, lover boy. So far from the truth.

"Oh, boy," I say dryly. "You've seen right through me. I want you. I need you. Oh, baby. Oh, baby."

That takes care of him. I'm ready to go. Only King Jerk (a.k.a. Joey Stupid) appears and blocks my car with his.

How did I get trapped in Loser Land?

"Hey, do you mind?" I call.

"Not at all," King Jerk replies. Then he heads into a store accompanied by his pumpkinhead posse.

I am not going to sit here and take this. I am not going to idle and wait with Stalker Man outside my window until King Jerk is done shopping for his size-0 jockstraps.

I am going to leave.

Joey's car is in the way?

Not a problem.

I rev the engine. I ram my nice fenders into Joey's precious door.

CRASH! — the sweetest sound.

Stalker Man looks pleased (points for him).

Joey looks the opposite of pleased.

I'm euphoric . . . until I get home and have to deal with my father . . . who is ballistic at the damage I've done to the car.

"Is this about Sarah Lawrence?" he yells. "Are you punishing me for wanting you to stay close to home?"

"Aren't *you* punishing *me* because Mom left?" I shoot back.

"This has nothing to do with her," he says. (Yeah, right.)

"Fine," I reply. "Then stop making my decisions for me."

He says that as my father, it's his right. (Who gave it to him? I certainly didn't.) What I want doesn't matter. He says I don't know what I want, and I won't know what I want until I'm forty-five.

Obviously, he's forgetting I'm me, not him. I know exactly what I want. And I tell him.

I want to go to an East Coast school. Away from here.

I want him to trust me to make my own choices.

I want him to stop trying to control my life just because he couldn't control my mother.

Does my father react? Does he even nod?

No. His beeper goes off and he leaves the room.

Cue Bianca. She walks in with this really *offended* look on her face.

"Did you just maim Joey's car?" she whines.

I tell her I guess she'll have to take the bus home now.

"Has the fact that you are completely psycho escaped your attention?" she screams. Then she calls out for "Daddy" and bolts out of the room.

I swear to Goddess, I may be many things, but I am *not* the psycho one in this family.

16
Patrick

Pretty Boy is having a fit. Kat just trashed his car. His date with Bianca isn't secure yet. His anger is rising.

It's time to hit him up for some more cash.

A hundred bucks now to date Kat. In advance.

He says to forget it, and I say he'll have to forget Kat's sister, then.

That shuts him up.

With him it isn't about love. It's about winning. And that's fine. With him, the desire to win is stronger than the desire to love.

So be it.

I take the money.

On to the next step.

17
Michael

Sometimes when a deal isn't working, you have to make other deals. I'm a dealmaker, so I understand how this works. Clearly, the simple Joey-pays-Patrick-to-date-the-shrew plan isn't working to its full potential. It's time to throw Cameron into the mix.

Cameron, of course, doesn't want to get too involved. He wants to spend all of his time mooning over fair Bianca. Which is a perfectly admirable thing to do. But sometimes you've got to crawl through some mud in order to be clean again.

We approach Patrick Verona at woodshop. I am relieved to see that he doesn't have a drill this time. I've brought my math book with me, just in case.

After a little hassle over who will actually talk to him, Cameron and I both make the approach. Cameron surprises me with a dead-on starter line:

"We know what you're trying to do with Kat Stratford."

We have Patrick's attention. "Is that right?" he sneers. "And what do you plan to do about it?"

"Help you out," Cameron says.

"Why's that?"

Cameron hesitates, and I step in. I tell Patrick that Cameron is crushing on Bianca. Patrick doesn't seem too surprised — he doesn't understand why everyone is falling for her, but that's fine with me, because the last thing in the world we need is for Mr. Long Hair to fall for *Bianca.*

Patrick makes some lewd remarks about Bianca's person, and Cameron gets all agitated. I assure Patrick that Cameron's love is pure. Much purer than, say, Joey Donner's.

Patrick shrugs and says he's only in it for the cash. Donner can be with whomever he wants.

Cameron objects strenuously. I'm seriously worried that he'll challenge Patrick to a duel.

"Patrick, Pat, let me explain," I say. "Joey's just a pawn. We set this whole thing up so *Cameron* can get the girl."

Patrick smiles at this. I can tell I've got him. He likes the idea of Joey being a pawn. He likes the idea that we're in control. I think.

I explain the deal: We're going to do some serious research, checking out what Kat likes and doesn't like. Then Patrick can take her to this big party Bogey is throwing Friday night and make his move.

"I'll think about it," Patrick replies.

But there's nothing to think about.

It's already done.

Of course, Bogey's party is supposed to be for Future MBAs only.

But I'll take care of that.

It doesn't take a whole lot of know-how to make up fake invitations.

And it's even easier to distribute them . . .

To everyone.

18
Bianca

Suddenly everyone is talking about Bogey's party on Friday night. I SO SO SO SO want to go. But will Daddy let me?

No — unless my witch sister has a date. ARRGH!

And I don't even want her to go just for *my* sake. I want her to go for *her* sake as well.

Joey is the first person to ask me about the party. We are standing in front of his locker. It's filled with pictures of his different modeling gigs. It's so sweet the way he shows them to me. The one where he's running in a field of daisies. The one where he's petting a kitten. Really sweet. He even shows me his headshots, and I tell him which one I like.

Then he asks me about Bogey's party. He says if I'm not going, he's not going to bother.

Isn't he the best?

Cameron is the next guy to ask me about the party. It's so cute how concerned he is about me. I tell him how I really, really want to go, but can't unless some fool takes Kat.

Cameron says he's taking care of it. Only so far Kat hasn't been going for the guy. I assure him that Kat has boy-crazy potential — I once found a picture of Jared Leto in one of her drawers.

"So that's the kind of guy she likes?" Cameron asks. "Pretty ones?"

"Who knows?" I say with a sigh. "All I've ever heard her say is that she'd die before dating a guy who smokes."

"All right. What else?"

"You're asking me to investigate the inner workings of my sister's twisted mind? Spooky!"

Cameron says nothing else has worked.

He says we need to go behind enemy lines.

That can mean only one thing: going into Kat's room.

The ick! The ick!

19

Cameron

I'm in Kat's room. I don't know what I was expecting — slaughtered chicken sacrifices, maybe? Black curtains, black sheets, a closet full of black clothes. Vampire gear.

But it isn't like that at all. And it isn't just because fair Bianca is beside me.

No, Kat's inner sanctum isn't a Nine Inch Nails video come to life. It's more than that.

Every inch of the walls is covered with something. Girl rocker posters, concert flyers, handwritten graffiti, random verses of poetry, Krazy Kat comics . . . it's amazing. Like Kat's personality has exploded in the middle of the room, sending fragments flying everywhere. The room is entirely, absolutely her own. After all my new-kid-in-town rooms of bare walls and lost-in-the-move posters, I have to respect that.

I gaze around hungrily. Everything I need is here in this room. Everything I need to know about Kat. She has put it up for everyone to see.

Only no one ever comes in.

No one is ever allowed.

After a few minutes, Bianca begins to get seriously nervous, and I have to leave. She doesn't want either Kat or her father to catch me in their house. I can't say I blame her. But at the same time, every ounce of my soul wants to stay. Just to stand in the hall, outside Bianca's room . . . perchance to breathe in her air . . . is pure bliss.

A bliss deferred, for now.

But every step I take now is one step closer to the time when we'll be together. I have to believe that.

Of course, it is not enough for me to see Kat's room. I have to make my report to Patrick as soon as possible. So that night Michael and I hop on Michael's motorcycle and head to a local dive bar, where Patrick plays pool with his buds.

Once we're inside the bar, I am floored. I mean, I have lived all over the country, but I've never really been in a bar before. Michael the expert — right — warns, "Don't touch anything. You may get hepatitis."

Overreact much?

Patrick is neither excited nor embarrassed to see us. He gets to the point right away, and asks what we've found out about Kat that could help him. I take his cigarette out of his mouth and say right off that Kat hates smokers.

"Are you telling me I'm a . . . *non-smoker*?!?" he gasps.

"Just for now," Michael assures him.

Then I state my second concern. Kat only goes for pretty guys.

"What?" Patrick asks. "You don't think I'm pretty?"

Michael slaps me on the head and says, "He's pretty!"

I say okay. I wasn't sure.

Next, I list Kat's other likes: Thai food, feminist prose, and angry girl music of the indie-rock persuasion. I hand over a list of the CDs in her room.

64

For a minute, I can see Patrick waver. "So I'm supposed to buy her some noodles and a book and sit around listening to chicks who can't play their instruments?" he asks.

Now, I think he's being a little unfair there, but it's not exactly the time to argue. I'm sure he'll get enough of that from Kat. So instead of debating the merits of Luscious Jackson, we tell Patrick that Kat's fave band is playing at Club Skunk tomorrow night. Kat will be there. Which means that Patrick needs to be there, too.

Patrick groans. "You might as well send me to Lilith Fair!" he protests.

But he's going to go. I can tell.

Deep down, he really wants to go.

Not because of the music.

Because of the challenge.

Because of her?

20
Kat

I'm conflicted. I am so *not* used to having something to look forward to. But the whole day, I can't help being excited. I will be seeing my favorite band tonight. At a small club, where no one from my school but me and Mandella would dare to show.

After we're released from prison for the day, Mandella and I dart downtown for some last-minute mascara. Then we head to my room and blast music to our heart's content. With every note, my anticipation grows.

Of course, Bianca has to interrupt the fun. She wants me to turn down the music because she's *studying.* How was I to know that she even did such a thing? How dare I disrupt it?

I make no move to turn down the music, so Bianca actually *comes into my room* and makes it softer.

"Do you mind?" I say. "We have someplace to be."

Bianca's mood unexpectedly morphs. "Oh, my God!" she cheers. "Does this mean you're becoming normal?"

"It means Kat's favorite band is playing Club Skunk and we're going," Mandella explains.

"Oh, right," Little Miss Student says coyly. "Have fun."

Will this be the end of her intrusion?

As if. There's more.

"I don't know why I'm bothering to ask," she begins (*Don't* bother, I want to yell), "but are you going to Bogey's party Friday night?"

"What do *you* think?" I reply. I mean, come on.

"I think you should attempt to interact with your peer group in an environment conducive to merriment," she prescribes.

"I'm about to," I tell her.

Merriment, here I come.

The club is jammed, but Mandella and I make our way to the front. The people around us are acting like fools. But I don't need that. I have the music.

From the first guitar assault, I am there. I can float away from all my worries and all my stress and just ride the music as it crashes through the air. Nobody stands in my way. Nobody can touch me.

I move. I sing the words. I sweat.

I am whole.

21
Patrick

Right in front of my eyes, Kat changes into this other person. Totally at ease. Defenses down.

Amazing.

22
Kat

I feel this unbelievable thirst. I need water. I need to take a break. I shout to Mandella and make my way to the bar.

Where Stalker Man is waiting.

I mean, *here* of all places. Invading my one perfect space.

I sneak a glance and catch him staring. He catches me glancing.

Damn.

I figure I have to attack this head-on. After I get my water, I march over to him.

I make it perfectly clear: If he's planning to ask me out again, he might as well get it over with.

I expect a typical Stalker Man comment. But instead he points to the band and gets all annoyed, saying, "Do you mind? You're sort of ruining it for me."

I'm ruining it for *him*? Excuse me?

Whatever. I point out that he's not surrounded by his usual Pigpen cloud of smoke.

"I know," he tells me. "I quit. Apparently, they're bad for you."

Okay, now we're entering the Twilight Zone.

"You think?" I say.

But he's not following the conversation. He's following the music.

"You know," he says, "these guys aren't Bikini Kill or the Raincoats, but they're not bad."

I can't believe it. *He* knows who the Raincoats are? I ask him and he says, "Why, don't you?"

What is going on?

I am so confused.

He leans over and brushes my hair back. It feels kind of . . . nice. He speaks right into my ear.

"I watched you out there," he says. "I've never seen you look like that before."

The music has stopped now. We don't have to yell.

I don't know what to say. I back away. If he says the right thing right now, I'll be in serious trouble.

Not to worry. He becomes Fake Smooth Guy again, going, "Come to Bogey's party with me."

The band starts to jam again. The noise returns.

"You never give up, do you?" I yell.

"So are you saying yes?" he asks.

"No." I turn away.

"Then are you saying no?" he shouts after me.

"No!" I yell.

Then he yells something back. But I'm gone by then. I'm back with the music.

I'm back from the verge of trouble.

23
Bianca

A day passes and suddenly it's Friday night and I *have* to go to Bogey's party. Everybody knows about it, although I'm not quite sure that Bogey knows that everybody knows about it. I have told Joey that I'm going to be there, whether or not Kat goes. That's my plan. Chastity comes home with me after school to help me in my getaway.

We try to tiptoe out. But Daddy catches me.

There's no way for me to explain. So I tell him I'm going to a small study group of friends, but since I can never lie to Daddy, he knows I'm fibbing. Chastity tries to tell him it's only a party, but that's the last thing Daddy wants to hear.

At this moment, Kat comes downstairs with her Walkman blaring, as if God wants to remind me why I can't go to the party. It doesn't matter that people expect me to be there. It doesn't matter that my sister will never go out on a date. It doesn't matter that IT'S MY LIFE AND I'M SICK AND TIRED OF BEING TOLD WHAT TO DO. (Where did that come from?)

I plead with my sister. Why can't she be normal? Why can't she just step out of her dimly lit Kat world for a moment and let me have fun for once in my life? I know she thinks Bogey's party is (and I quote) "a lame excuse for all the idiots in our school to drink beer and rub up against each other in hopes of distracting themselves from the pathetic emptiness of their meaningless, consumer-driven lives." I know she thinks I'm one of those idiots, and no matter how hard I try, I'll never persuade her otherwise. I know she thinks she's above us all. But still, I have to ask, "Can't you, for just one night, forget that you're completely wretched and be my sister?"

I'm totally begging her. I know it's just a single stupid party, but it's really much more than that. If I can't go now, I don't know if I'll ever be able to go. I will live my whole life waiting for my life to begin.

Kat just looks at me for a second. Doesn't she know how it feels? Doesn't one tiny itty-bit of her soul know what it's like to want to go out?

Suddenly, she's all, "If I go, will you cease your endless whining?"

"Duh," Chastity answers for me.

"Fine," Kat states. "I'll make an appearance."

I can't believe it!

I! Am! So! Happy!

Chastity and I are in heaven.

Daddy now looks as gloomy as Kat. "Oh, God," he groans. "It's starting."

I assure him it's only a party.

But that's not enough for him.

He wants me to wear . . . *the belly.*

The big, hideous belly that makes you feel like you're pregnant. I mean, it's like strapping a sack of flour to your stomach. When I put it on, I look like a reject Tele-tubby.

At first, I think he wants me to wear it to the party. Then, thank God, he says he only wants me to wear it around the living room for a minute, so I can "realize the weight of my decisions."

As if I don't already know.

Believe me, I know.

I love Daddy to death, but he's completely imbalanced. I think he could have handled sons much better.

Kat, of course, doesn't have to wear the belly. While I waddle around, she heads right to the door. Daddy shouts out warnings to her.

Then we all get a surprise.

Kat opens the door, and there's a cute boy waiting.

For her.

We're all having a race to see who will have the first heart attack: me, Daddy, Chastity, or Kat.

Only the guy seems calm.

"Nine-thirty, right?" he says in a totally hot accent. "I'm early."

"Whatever," Kat grunts. "I'm driving."

She's trying to act all cool. But I can tell. She's flustered.

I never thought I'd see the day!

Daddy doesn't say a word. I hand him back the belly, and Chastity and I head out.

It's time for me to begin my new, happy life.

Joey is waiting.

24
Cameron

There are two approaches to going to a party. One approach is to try to make yourself into someone you're not. Michael is taking this approach, which invariably ends up saying much more about you than you want anyone to know. He's splashing on too much cologne and wearing this out-of-control (or perhaps too-much-in-control) suit and tie. I try to tell him to ease up, but that only makes him more nervous.

The other approach is the one I'm trying to use: Instead of trying to be someone you're not, you can simply try to emphasize who you really are. I think Bianca will like this approach much more. I don't want her to be fake with me, and I don't want to be fake with her. I don't want any lies or wrong expectations to get between us.

I am nervous, but my nervousness is quieter than Michael's. I can't help but think aloud about the last conversation I had with Bianca. I told her that her blue shoes might have gone better with her outfit than the black ones she was wearing, and she said that she almost didn't wear the Kenneth Coles because she thought she was mixing, you know, genres. And the fact that I noticed this small fact about her outfit — and I'm quoting here — "really meant something."

That's all I want out of life — to really mean something to her.

Michael has heard this a thousand times by now. He wants me to focus on *him* for a second and how he looks. I tell him to ditch his tie — it makes him look like my uncle Milt.

"I'm so nervous," he says. "The last party I went to was at Chuck E. Cheese."

I try to calm him down. I tell him the party will be fun.

After all, it's not the party I'm nervous about.

I pray with all my heart that Bianca will be there.

25
Kat

Poor Bogey. I can tell from the brie on the ceiling and the Merlot stains on the couch that he'd intended this to be a quiet wine-and-cheese affair. Now it's all drunken chaos, with high school bodies pulsing, thumping, and yelling. The air is full of beer and sound. The furniture will never recover.

I'd feel bad for Bogey, if he didn't deserve it so much.

I push through the crowd, with Patrick Stalker Man somewhere on my trail. In the dining-room jock-crowd hell, King Jerk Joey catches me off guard. I try to get away, but he blocks the doorway.

"Lookin' fresh tonight," he burps. I could

not be more repulsed. All these bad memories come back to me.

I shoot him a death look and point at his forehead.

"Wait," I say. "Was that? Did your hairline just recede?"

I have to strike at his vanity. It's his biggest target.

While he ponders what I've said, I turn to go.

"Where're you going?" he asks. He is so gone.

"Away," I state flatly.

"Your sister here?"

He knows just which button to push. Now he's got me started. I am feeling total hatred.

"Stay away from my sister," I warn him, ice-picking every word into his small, small brain.

He smirks. "Sure, I'll stay away from your sister. But I can't guarantee she'll stay away from me."

A fight breaks out in the next room. The mothership has called Joey now, and he lunges for the pummeling. I make my escape. I can hear the hooting of violent spectators. I hear someone going through a window. I pray that it's Joey, and that somehow he's fallen to his death, even though we're only on the first floor.

But I'm not so lucky.

A short time later, Joey reappears.

I am walking through the sitting room and I see him there. Talking to Bianca.

"Look who found me," he gloats. He puts his arms around her and escorts her out.

I can't stand it. This can't happen. I grab her arm and drag her back.

"Bianca, wait —" I say.

But she's shut down. I've already lost her. "Please do not address me in public," she condescends.

I want to explain to her. I know things she doesn't. I need to tell her something.

But she won't let me.

"I am busy enjoying my adolescence," she declares. "So scamper off and do the same."

She heads out. Joey smirks and says "ba bye" to me.

The scum.

The total pond scum.

The Padua High crowd: the fair Bianca in the middle, surrounded by [bottom, l. to r.] Cameron, Joey, Michael, and [top, l. to r.] Kat, Patrick, and Chastity.

She really *is* all that — it's love at first sight when Cameron [left] sees Bianca. Michael's advice? "Don't even think about it."

Bianca needs a French tutor. Besotted Cameron volunteers. "You speak French?" Michael inquires. "No, but I will," Cameron replies.

Alas, Cameron and Bianca can't date —
because older sister Kat [left] refuses to even
consider going out with any of the "unwashed
miscreants" at school. And Daddy's rule is,
Bianca can't date until Kat does. Problemo!

Cameron asks tough dude Patrick [right] to *please* date Kat.

Obnoxious rich kid Joey [right] *pays* Patrick to date Kat — so *he* can go out with Bianca.

Cameron tells Bianca he's found someone to date Kat. "Is he demented?" she asks. "You bet," Cameron answers. "He sounds perfect," she decides.

Prom night, and the plan has worked. As a confused Daddy looks on, Cameron picks up his beautiful Bianca.

But when Patrick is forced to confess to Kat that he dated her — at first — for the money, it *doesn't* end well. She never hears the words "at first."

Patrick plays the fool to win back Kat's love. On the soccer field bleachers, he croons, "Can't Take My Eyes Off of You." She is mortified! Also, touched!

After a paintball battle royal, Kat recites a poem to Patrick. It details all the ways she detests him — and ends thusly: "But mostly I hate the way I don't hate you. Not even a little bit. Not even at all."

Some anonymous MBA guy brings over a tray of shots.

Since my life is already out of control, I decide to down a few.

Patrick comes over and says he's been looking all over for me. He asks me what I'm doing.

I tell him I'm "getting trashed, man." What everyone expects you to do at a party.

Patrick tells me to do what I want to do.

I tell him he's the only one who feels that way.

But I plan to listen to him anyway.

26
Cameron

The chaos is amazing. The wreckage grows by the hour. It's like a FOX TV special — *When Disaster Strikes Dining Rooms*. I must find Bianca. I am a ship in a storm, and she is my only possible beacon.

Michael loves the chaos and the totally damaged look on Bogey's face. Unfortunately, he's been a little less lucky in the love department. He thinks it's because he ditched the tie. I don't have the heart to tell him it's not.

Finally, halfway through the party, I see her. She is walking down the stairway with her friend Chastity.

I have never seen her more beautiful.

"Hey, Bianca!" I call.

"Oh, hi, Cameron," she says.

She asks me if I know Chastity, and I say, yeah, I think we have art together. Chastity doesn't seem that interested.

I tell Bianca she looks amazing.

She says thanks.

And then Joey steps in, saying, "And we all know that *I* look amazing."

Why oh why did he ever have to be born?

No one except Chastity laughs. I take this as a good sign.

Then Joey takes Bianca's arm and says they have to go.

"I'll see you around, okay?" Bianca says.

Joey shoots me a triumphant look.

And then she's gone.

I've lost her.

It's over.

My beacon is gone and I'm drowning now. The storm is all around me and I can't even save myself. I don't even know if I want to.

She's gone.

27
Bianca

I'm *finally* where I want to be, with the guy I want to be with, and everything's . . . um . . . not so great. It's like, you know, Joey puts his hand on my arm and leads me to the living room. And it's strange, because his hand on my arm feels like . . . a hand on my arm. And when you're being touched by the guy that you like, it should feel like much more than just a hand on an arm.

Joey sips from a beer and talks about himself. And (help me!) his modeling.

"I've got the Sears catalog thing going," he tells me (and everyone else who wants to listen). "And the tube sock gig — that's gonna be huge. Then I'm up for a hemorrhoid cream ad next week. That should be cool, 'cause I'll get to do some acting."

And suddenly I'm getting to do a little acting of my own. I act like I'm interested.

I'm still waiting for the fun part to begin.

The pyramid of empty beer cans gets taller. Joey goes from talking about his ads to acting them out. He shows me the tube sock pose and the khakis pose and the turtleneck pose. Then he shows me the underwear pose and the bathing suit pose — they're exactly the same, but somehow Joey thinks they're different. Maybe he's just too subtle for me?

I don't think so.

This is so NOT HOW I THOUGHT TONIGHT WOULD BE.

While pretending to still be with him, I frantically search the room for Chastity. Through the magic of best friend telepathy, she walks in the door and I catch her eye. We make an excuse and say we have to go to the ladies' room.

Guys always wonder why girls go to the bathroom in pairs. Well, the truth is we're usually just trying to get away from them.

87

The bathroom has somehow survived the party so far. I can actually enter without worrying about where I step. Immediately, I shut the door and groan about my evening with Mr. Tube Sock. He is *so* boring!

"Joey practically peed himself when he found out that we have the same dermatologist," I tell Chastity. "I mean, Dr. Bonchowski is great and all, but he's not exactly relevant party conversation."

"Is he oily or dry?" Chastity asks.

"Combination," I reply. Then I shift away from skin problems. I tell her that sometimes I wonder if the guys we're supposed to want to go out with are the ones we *actually* want to go out with.

"Can we step back into the real world for a second?" Chastity goes. "You don't go out with Joeys for enjoyment. You go out with them to be *seen.*"

I guess I know what she means. I would've said the same thing to her if she was in my position.

But now, all of a sudden, it doesn't seem to work right.

I'm not so sure I want to step back into the real world.

Not if Joey's the best I can do.

There's a knock at the door. Since it's totally uncool to monopolize a bathroom during a party, I open the door — and find my sister. This time she's not just obnoxious. She's out of her head.

She rails into me right away, saying she needs to talk to me.

I can only imagine what she'll say. I'm not in the mood for a lecture about the pointlessness of existence right now.

I tell her to save it for later. She's totally Cuervoed.

And I'm totally exiting.

I push my way through the house with Chastity right behind me. I see Cowboys spitting into vases and Joey still posing for a whole set of drooly girls. Bottles and puddles are everywhere. I just want to get out. I see Cameron and our eyes meet for a second. Then he disappears, looking hurt.

What's going on?

The party isn't really that different than it was an hour ago. Except all of a sudden, it sucks.

And I am entirely over it.

I want something else.

28
Patrick

Some people just can't handle a party.

I never would have expected Kat to be one of them.

I keep finding her and losing her. And every time I find her again, she's further gone.

I try to take the shot glass from her hand. She protests. She says she wants another one.

Then Pretty Boy Joey comes in and distracts me. He asks me how I got her to act like a human. I want to point out to him that she was human all along, but I've lost his attention. Instead, he's focusing on Kat, who's jumped onto a pool table.

To dance.

By herself.

She's letting loose, and everyone is watching. They're hooting at her and cheering her on.

I can't stand it.

She swings her head around and bangs it on a lamp. I rush to catch her. People clap, thinking it's part of the act. It's tempting to not get involved.

But I am. Involved.

I set her down on her feet and ask her if she's okay.

"I'm fine," she replies, trying to push me away. But she doesn't have the strength.

"You're not okay," I point out.

"I just need to lie down for a while," she says.

I tell her she needs to walk it off. She might even have a concussion.

After I get her out into the night air, someone grabs my arm. I'm ready for a fight. But it's only that kid Cameron.

He says we need to talk. I point out that I'm a little busy.

"It's off," Cameron says, and for the first time I can see the total heartbreak on his face. "Bianca doesn't want me. She wants Joey."

I don't have time for this. I've managed to get Kat to sit down, but she won't stay there forever.

"Cameron," I say plainly, "do you like this girl?"

"Yeah."

"Is she worth the trouble?" I ask.

"I thought she was —"

"Either she is, or she isn't," I tell him. "So give it a shot, or don't give it a shot. But either way, don't let anyone make you feel like you don't deserve what you want. Remember that."

Kat slides off the chair. I pick her up and continue to walk her around.

I don't look back at Cameron.

Either he's going to listen, or he won't.

Either he loves her, or he doesn't.

Things don't always have to be so complicated.

29
Cameron

What do I do?

30
Kat

Part of me is walking with Patrick Stalker Man and part of me is so incredibly tired that I just want to pass out on my feet. I find it *so* patronizing to be led around by some guy.

Why is he doing this? Who would want to be with me right now?

WHAT IS WRONG WITH HIM?

"Why're you doing this?" I slur.

"I told you. You might have a concussion."

"You don't care if I never wake up."

"Sure I do."

"Why?" I have to ask.

"Because then I'd have to start taking out girls who actually like me."

"Like you can find one," I snort.

"See that? Who needs affection when I've got blind hatred?"

Maybe it's too mean to say what I said. I said it, but I'm not sure I wanted to say it. I don't know. All I want to do is sit down.

He puts me on a swing and I fall right off.

My body is particularly susceptible to gravity right now.

Patrick puts me back on (so patronizing!) and starts to push me on the swing.

Like what I really need is movement.

"Why'd you let him get to you?" he asks.

"Who?" I ask.

"Joey."

"I hate him." That's clear enough. No need to go into the details.

We say something else, and then I'm totally asleep. Patrick shakes me hard and I wake up again. His eyes have a little green in them. We stare at each other for a moment.

Then I puke.

He probably shouldn't have pushed me on the swing.

31
Bianca

Sometimes your life changes and it's totally out of your control. Like when your mother decides to leave you so she can be with a med student. Or when your sister crashes the car and your father starts thinking that maybe *you* shouldn't get a license after all.

Sometimes, though, you have a say in where your life is going to go. Sometimes you make a really big decision, and even though you might not know that it's really big at the time, it ends up being just as important as what everybody else does.

Chastity and I are walking outside when Joey catches up to us. He says a bunch of people are going to Jaret's house. He wants us to come.

But he doesn't say, "Do you want to go?" or "I'd really love you to join me" or anything like that.

No — he says, "Let's go."

His decision.

I make one, too.

I decide I've had it.

I put on my best pained expression and say I have to be home in twenty minutes.

Then Chastity shocks me by saying *she's* free until two!

"One more chance," Joey goes.

I don't take it.

Chastity does.

She leaves me standing alone in the yard.

Some best friend.

As Chastity chases after Joey, Cameron comes by.

"Have fun tonight?" he asks. There's something in his voice that I have never heard before. It's almost like anger.

"Tons," I tell him. He starts to walk away.

But I don't want him to go. I don't want to be all alone.

I ask him if he can give me a ride home. He doesn't even have to say a word. His expression is clearly a yes.

32
Cameron

Hope!

99

33
Patrick

No way am I going to let Kat drive herself home. So I shift her toward the passenger side of her car and take her keys.

She's been on mute since the whole swing set mess. Now she slumps in the car seat. Once we're going, she fiddles with the radio until some rock chick comes on.

I change the station and tell her *I* get to pick the tunes, since I'm driving.

She changes the station back and says *she* gets to pick the tunes, since it's her car.

But I'm in control of it. So I turn back to my station.

But it's that band that she's been listening to. And I'm supposed to like them, since I was at their concert.

She wins. The station is hers.

I think this is going to be the end of our conversation, but she surprises me.

"When you were gone last year — where were you?" she asks. It's the great unspoken question.

"Busy," I say.

"Were you in jail?"

"Maybe."

"No you weren't," she says.

"Then why'd you ask?"

"Why'd you lie?"

Doesn't she get it? Sometimes lies are the only protection you have.

I turn up the radio — why not? She points to it and bobs her head, saying, "I should do that."

"Start a band?" I guess.

She gets all sarcastic. "No, install car stereos." Then she calms down. "Yeah, start a band. My father would looooooove that."

We're in front of her house now. I turn off the ignition.

"You don't strike me as the type that asks permission," I note.

She turns to look at me straight-on. "Oh, so now you think you know me?"

"I'm getting there."

I expect her to shoot back. But instead she quiets down.

"The only thing people know about me is that I'm 'scary,'" she says. She doesn't seem scary right now, but I'm afraid to tell her that.

I tell her I'm no picnic myself.

We're sort of alike.

I look at her near-silent house and ask her what the deal is with her father. She says he wants her to be someone she's not. I ask her who he wants her to be.

"Bianca," is her answer.

"No offense," I say, "I know everyone digs her, but your sister is *without*."

She looks at me with something approaching admiration.

"You know," she confesses, "you're not as vile as I thought you were."

Then she leans in for a kiss.

I want it, but not like this.

At the last second, I turn away.

102

"Maybe we should do this another time," I say.

She stares at me, hurt.

Then, before I can explain, she runs away.

34
Cameron

We pull up to Bianca's house just as a car pulls away. I barely notice, I'm so confused. I love Bianca and I'm angry at her and I'm hurt by her and I'm hopeful about her. Does that make sense?

"You never wanted to go sailing with me, did you?" I ask.

"Yes, I did," she answers. But I can tell she's lying.

"No, you didn't," I protest.

And I get the truth: "Well, no, not actually, but —"

I tell her that's all she had to say.

"But —" she sputters.

"Have you always been this selfish?" I can't stop myself from saying it.

She pauses for a long minute. Then, quietly, she says, "Yes."

I don't know where I find the words. But somehow I do. I tell her that she can't treat people like they don't matter, just because she's beautiful. I tell her I really liked her. I tell her I defended her when people said she was conceited. I helped her when she asked me to. I even learned French for her. And then she just blew me off, so she could —

I get no further.

Her kiss stops me.

Entirely unexpected. And then there she is. And my lips are touching her lips, and all of my anger melts away. Because she's not kissing me to shut me up. She's kissing me because she understands.

I kiss her back.

It's wonderful.

When we stop, she smiles, surprised at herself. Then she gets out of the car and glides to her doorway.

I grin.

I am back in the game.

35
Kat

What have I done?

I spent the weekend in blissful denial, avoiding the real world and the King Jerks that walk within it.

Now I'm forced back into prison. And all the other inmates are giving me grief, reminding me of my party-going exploits — which, to be honest, I don't remember too well myself.

"Kat, my lady, you sway to the rhythm of my heart," one of the White Rastas says.

"Dance for me, cowgirl!" one of the Cowboys calls out.

I want to sink into the floor.

Then Mr. Morgan gets on my case for no apparent reason. I have the gall to actually

say I *want* to do one of his assignments —
we're supposed to write a poem — and he
kicks me out of the room, with Joey Donner
gloating the whole time.

I get to Ms. Perky's office and find Big
Rat Patrick Stalker Man there.

"You two know each other?" Ms. Any-
thing-But asks in horror.

I say no.

Loser Boy says yes.

I can't stand him. I can't stand the sight
of him. I can't believe I once thought — I'm
so over it.

Ms. Perky tells him to stay away from
me. (The first time we've ever agreed on
anything!)

He grins at me. I glare at him.

Could this day get any worse?

36

Michael

Bianca tells Chastity who tells Joey who
tells one of his henchman who tells me that
Patrick wasn't exactly successful in his court-
ship of Kat on Friday night.

It's time to get more information.

Cameron is floating around like a happy
balloon, and I don't want to see him popped.

So I go directly to the source. Not to
Kat — that would be suicide.

But her friend Mandella is a lot nicer.

I catch her at her locker. It's decked out
with all kinds of Shakespeare pinups.

"Cool pictures," I say, pointing to a cou-
ple of portraits. "What's that collar for? To
keep him from licking his stitches?"

It's a joke, but Mandella's not going for it.

"Kidding," I say. "I know you're a fan of Shakespeare."

"More than a fan," she states dramatically. "We're *involved.*"

I decide to open up my own can of Willie and quote, "'*Who could refrain that had a heart to love, and in that heart —*'"

"'*— courage to make's love known?*'" she concludes, happily stunned.

"*Macbeth*, right?" I say.

"Right," she replies, still dazed.

Now that I have her attention, I lean in a little closer.

"So listen," I say. "I have this friend . . . and he likes your friend . . ."

Yes, it's more third-grade romance than unabridged Shakespeare.

But it gets the job done.

Forsooth.

37

Cameron

I fear that it was just a dream. An incredible, vivid dream. Did her lips really touch mine? Could she possibly care for me in the way that I care for her?

We pass each other in the hallways, and she gives me a secret, knowing smile.

It wasn't a dream. And it's still a dream.

If only Kat were as happy as we are. My worst fear is that she'll refuse to date again. Mr. Stratford will keep Bianca locked in their house, unable to see me again.

Despair!

And yet . . .

I saw Patrick and Kat together at the party. I'd swear there was something there.

But what do I know?

After school, Patrick and I sit in the bleachers as Kat practices soccer. She will not look at us. Or, more to the point, she won't look at *him*. Me, I'm invisible.

"What'd you do to her?" I ask. If it's his fault, I'll . . . oh, I don't know what I'll do.

"I didn't do anything," he says. "She would've been too drunk to remember it."

"Look," I tell him, "this plan was working —"

"What do you care? I thought you wanted out."

I tell him I did — until Bianca kissed me.

He raises his eyebrow and asks me where.

"In the car," I say. And that's all I'll say. It seems wrong to be talking about it.

Michael runs across the field to talk to us. He's gotten the full scoop from Kat's best friend. Apparently, Kat hates Patrick "with the fire of a thousand suns."

That's pretty bad.

"Maybe she just needs a day to cool off," I offer.

Then Kat sends a soccer ball flying at Patrick's head.

"Maybe two," Patrick replies.

My dream is turning into a nightmare.

38

Kat

Thank Goddess for Mandella. Sometimes I think she's the only person in this whole town who has even a remote clue about who I am. She and I go over the whole Big Rat Patrick Stalker Man thing, and she agrees with me — he's a freak. And not a very good one at that.

As I walk through the prison corridors, I notice that it has been decorated lately with posters advertising the prom — the high school equivalent of *Dead Man Walking.* I rip down the posters whenever I get a chance. This time I show one to Mandella and ask her if she can even *imagine* going to such an antiquated mating ritual.

She sort of looks down at the floor and says that, actually, um, she would go, if she had a date.

Excuse me?

"All right, all right," she says. "We won't go. It's not like I have a dress anyway."

I tell her she's looking at this from the wrong perspective. Really, we're making a *statement* by not going.

"Oh, good," Mandella deadpans. "Something new and different for us."

I don't know what to say. I guess I forget that Mandella sometimes wants to do normal things. I guess it's just her nice streak manifesting itself in strange ways.

I don't know how she puts up with me.

When it comes to normal, I'm absolutely no help.

39

Bianca

I avoid Joey like a bad hair day. I have absolutely nothing to say to him, and I KNOW he has absolutely nothing to say to me. He just doesn't realize it. Maybe because he's so used to having nothing to say.

I don't really talk to Cameron, either. But that's a different kind of not talking. With him, it's like we're talking even when we're not. When we say something to each other, we want it to really count. It has to be special. Or something like that.

I still don't know why I kissed him in the car.

But I'm kind of glad I did.

Unfortunately, Joey still finds a way to interfere with my thoughts. He catches me in gym class, when I'm lethally armed with a bow and arrow.

I hate coed gym. You can never get anything done.

"Hey there, Cupid," he calls.

"Hey, Joey," I reply coolly, still looking at the target, trying to find some logic in the arrangement of the bull's-eye colors.

"You're concentrating awfully hard, considering it's gym class," he goes on.

I glance at Joey and let go of the arrow. I hear a cry and turn back to the target. Apparently, I've hit Mr. Chapin, the gym teacher, instead.

Oops.

Joey's all, "I wanna talk to you about the prom."

For the first time in my whole entire life, I am thankful for Daddy's stupid rule.

"You know the deal," I tell Joey, *faux* upset. "I can't go if Kat doesn't go."

"Your sister *is* going."

Whoa — news flash.

"Since when?" I ask.

Joey takes the bow and arrow out of my hand and makes a Cupid gesture.

"Let's just say I'm taking care of it," he says.

Help!

40
Patrick

Joey must be getting desperate. He's upping the price. Three hundred dollars to take Kat to the prom.

Three hundred dollars, man.

And I don't want it.

I tell Joey — I'm tired of his little game.

Suddenly, it seems wrong.

But Joey insists.

So then I figure I can use the money to do some good. Besides, it would be a shame for *Joey* to keep it.

So I take it.

But I want to make this clear — it's not about money anymore.

It's about Kat.

I'm going all out.

I know she hates me . . . but that kind of hate can change into . . .

I don't want to say it.

So my campaign to win Kat's heart begins again in earnest.

I find her in the local guitar store. She is trying out a Stratocaster — it's almost as beautiful as she is. She plugs in her headphones and closes her eyes. I can tell she's lost in the music, lost in the notes that her fingers choose. I walk up right next to her. She is enraptured, in this private, wonderful place. I can read it on her face. I am so close — but I can't say a word. There isn't a single thing I could say that would equal what she's feeling right now. The best thing I can do is leave her alone.

She'll never even know I was there.

The next day we're in a bookstore together. I go to the salesperson and ask for a copy of *The Feminine Mystique.* I even say I lost my old copy — so Kat will think I've already read it.

Kat is flustered by my appearance. She asks me what I'm doing here, and I tell her I heard there was a poetry reading. It's the first time we've talked face-to-face since Ms. Perky's office.

"You're so —" Kat says.

"Charming?" I try. "Wholesome?"

"*Unwelcome.*"

Her anger is becoming flirtatious.

I lean close, twisting a strand of her hair around my finger.

"You're not as mean as you think you are, you know," I tell her.

She smacks my hand away . . . and it goes downhill from there.

The next day in the cafeteria, Cameron and Michael flank me, eager for good news.

I wish I had some to give them.

I tell them they're right — Kat is still angry.

"Sweet love, renew thy force!" Michael exclaims.

I tell him to keep his voice down. I mean, people can *hear* him.

Cameron says that since I embarrassed Kat by not kissing her, I need to sacrifice myself on the altar of dignity and even the score.

I walk away at that point. That's just stupid.

And then I realize it's also right.

I can be as cool as I want around Kat — she won't be impressed.

But if I make a total fool of myself, she might realize what's really going on.

She might begin to understand how I really feel.

I'm just beginning to understand it myself.

41
Kat

Soccer practice is probably the only part of prison that I willingly submit to. This is because the other girls on my team actually have minds of their own, and they're not afraid to use them. A few "Mallruses" usually join up at the beginning of the year, but by the time we get through with them, they're lean, mean, kicking machines who don't even mind taking off their earrings to play.

I have never been accused of being a team player, but soccer is the only time I really try. I've managed to earn a little respect among my teammates. And I'm proud of that.

So imagine my reaction when, during

soccer practice, a certain song starts playing over the loudspeakers. The field is entirely full of people. Guys are running track. The marching band is practicing their two-step. Boyfriends, girlfriends, and smokers loiter in the stands.

And suddenly a voice is singing this old love ballad.

"Can't Take My Eyes Off of You."

Of course, I immediately feel sorry for whoever's doing the singing. He's pretty bad.

I feel even more sorry for the girl he's singing to. I wonder which of my teammates it is.

We all look up at the announcer's booth. The door opens.

Patrick walks out.

I. Am. Mortified.

If he tries to pull me up to the bleachers, I will kill him.

But he doesn't. He's committed to his song, even if he can't hit all the notes.

I'm so murderously angry at him.

Only . . . I'm not.

I'm feeling it now. The hate is all going away. I want to hide, but at the same time I'm glad I'm here. Because Patrick is making a complete fool of himself. And he's doing it for me.

How could I not be touched? I'd have to be made of stone. And, contrary to popular opinion, I'm not.

Everybody's watching him now, cheering him on. The marching band starts to play along. It's one of those bizarre moments when everything is in harmony.

He looks at me and I look right back.

A smile lights up his face.

Then the school security guard takes him away.

My Big Rat Stalker Man Love Crooner.

I'll have to save him.

42
Patrick

You'd think that breaking into the announcer's booth and splicing the audio system was a crime or something. And maybe it
is. But I did it with the noblest of intentions.
I don't think I should be given detention
for it.

But I guess that's how the world works.

Mr. Chapin is one of those power trip detention monitors. He always volunteers to
stay after school because there's nothing
really for him to go home to. So instead of
catching *Oprah*, he confiscates Chee•tos
and other substances from nervous,
squirming students.

I'm ready to endure two whole hours of
this painful classroom monotony when Kat

walks into the room. At first, I'm thinking she has detention, too. But no. Instead, she's come to talk to Mr. Chapin.

I hear her mention something about the soccer team. I wonder if she even knows I'm in the room. Then she looks over to me and moves her head. I shrug — I have no idea what she's talking about. Or if she's trying to signal me.

Then she stares at the window, and I get it. She wants me to make a break for it!

This is a first. *She's* rescuing *me*. Or, at least, attempting to.

Kat grabs Mr. Chapin's arm and turns him away from the window. I slide out of my seat and head over. A few times I have to stop, because it looks like Mr. Chapin will catch me. But Kat's in control of the situation. I stop looking at them and make my way out the window.

And all the while, I can't stop thinking: She likes me. She really, really likes me.

Very cool.

I wait for her by her car. She comes out of the school and heads right over. Like she knew where I'd be. We didn't even have to discuss it.

We drive over to MacArthur Park and take out a paddleboat. It's like the air is finally clear between us. We're not throwing out any interference. We're not surrounding ourselves with anger or banter or evasion. It's just the two of us. As we are.

I tell her I can't thank her enough for helping me sneak out. She says it was no problem.

"I thought for sure I was busted when I was crawling out the window," I confess. "How'd you keep him distracted?"

"I dazzled him with my wits," she replies. Whatever works, I guess.

Now I want to talk about other things.

"So," I say. "What's your excuse?"

"For?"

"Acting the way we do."

Because it's clear we act the same way.

"I don't like to do what people expect," Kat says. "Why should I live up to their expectations instead of my own?"

"So if you disappoint them from the start, you're covered?" I guess. (It all sounds very familiar.)

"Something like that."

"Then you screwed up," I say.

"How?"

"You never disappointed me."

She blushes. It's the sweetest sight.

We're back at the dock and have to figure out what to do next.

Inspiration hits me.

"You up for it?" I ask.

"Up for what?" she says.

I point to a nearby sign.

Advertising paintball.

43
Kat

He is SO WEIRD.

I like that.

We get into this massive mega-paintball war. I swear I've never had more fun. And the miracle is that I actually realize I'm having fun. A retro sensation.

We're not into the whole I-like-you-so-I'm-going-to-let-you-win crap. No, we go after each other full-force, nailing each other with big glops of paint. It is so messy and it is so fun and I can't stop laughing and shooting and tracking him down.

Finally, we've run out of ammo, and we're entirely covered. He grabs me in a victorious tackle, and I grab back. We land on the ground and laugh.

Then things get all quiet. We are looking one another right in the eye. There is nothing between us, except about seventeen layers of paint.

He wipes a smear of blue paint from my lips and leans closer.

That is the calm.

The kiss is the storm.

44
Patrick

We're still covered in paint when we get back to Kat's house. Which is kind of ironic, since our conversation is scraping the layers off. We are peeling off all the attitude and the reputation and getting down to who we really are.

"None of that stuff is true," I confess about the rumors as we walk to her front porch.

"State trooper?" she asks.

Nope. I didn't kill a state trooper.

Did *she* kill someone in the parking lot?

Nope. Just a rumor.

"The duck?" Kat asks.

"Hearsay," I say. (I don't even like duck — why would I eat a whole one?)

Bobby Ridgeway?

"Fact," Kat states without remorse. "But he deserved it. He groped me in the lunch line."

Sounds fair enough to me.

Next she asks me about my accent, and I tell her it's real.

I tell her I lived in Australia until I was ten.

"With the Pygmies?" she asks.

"Close," I say. "With my mum."

We're on the porch steps now. I lean over and kiss her neck. It tickles her, and she laughs.

"Tell me something true," she says.

"I hate peas," I confess.

"No." She's serious now when she speaks. "Something real. Something no one else knows."

I tell her she's sweet. And sexy. And hot for me.

No one else knows that.

I can tell I'm getting through.

She says she can't believe I could fall for her (or words to that effect). Then she asks what's in it for me.

"Nothing," I say. "There's nothing in it for me. Just the pleasure of your company."

It's my only lie of the night.

I wish the money had never happened.

I'm so beyond that now.

45
Bianca

Cameron is taking his time about asking
me to the prom. We still rendezvous — I
learned a word! — for French lessons, but
our conversations go something like this:

"May I offer you a parsnip?"

"No, you may not."

"Where is my uncle's pencil?"

"I don't know."

When I ask him, *Laisse moite demander
une question, Cameron. Quand me deman-
deras tu de sortir avec toi?"* ("Let me ask
you a question, Cameron. When are you going to ask me out?") he scrambles for a dic-
tionary.

Sigh.

In the meantime, I have to deal with Daddy.

I wait until the night before the prom. I catch Daddy when he's exercising, because that's always a very vulnerable time for him.

"Daddy," I say, keeping my voice very direct, "I'd like to discuss tomorrow night with you. As you know, it's the prom."

"The prom?" he replies, playing dumb. Then he wises up. "The prom is tomorrow night! Kat has a date?"

Well, no. I start to explain this, but Daddy cuts me off.

"Don't think you're fooling me for a second," he says. "I know who you want me to bend the rules for. It's that hot rod Joey."

"What's a 'hot rod'?" I ask. It sounds totally *Grease*.

But Daddy doesn't tell me. Instead he lays down the law and says I'm not going unless Kat goes. End of story.

"Okay," I say. "Let's review. Kat? Not interested. Me? Dying to go." It doesn't seem fair that we should be judged on the same scale. It's like saying Kat can't stop shaving her legs until I do. Which would be, like, never.

"You know what happens at proms?" Daddy asks.

Oh, no, I think. *Here we go again.*

"Yes, Daddy." I try to keep my voice calm. "We'll dance. We'll kiss. We'll come home. It's not quite the crisis situation you imagine."

But no. My Baby Doctor Daddy can't imagine that something as innocent as just *kissing* would happen. No, he assumes the worst. He gives me absolutely positively no credit, and I swear I want to die from frustration.

"Can we for two seconds ignore the fact that you are severely unhinged and discuss my need for a night of teenage normalcy?" I plead, my voice getting a little angry.

"And what's normal?" Daddy asks. "Those damn *Dawson's Creek* kids, sleeping in each other's beds and whatnot?"

I start to protest that this isn't exactly a Dawson-Joey situation, but Daddy plows on.

"Oh, I'm *down,*" he proclaims, in a manner which definitely isn't down. "I've got the 411. And you are not going out and getting jiggy with some boy. I don't care how dope his ride is."

ARRGH!

I CAN'T TAKE IT ANYMORE!

I AM SO FED UP WITH THIS!

I storm out of the room before I say something that I'll really regret later, like YOU ARE THE WORST DADDY IN THE WORLD or NOW I KNOW WHY MOMMY LEFT!

Oh, my God. I can't believe I even thought that.

I am just going to go back to my room, turn on MTV, and try to think of a way out of this mess.

I am so sick of my life.

No — that's not true.

I'm just sick of my family.

46
Kat

I hear Bianca's door slam and figure things didn't exactly go well with our father.

It's time we had a talk.

I know I'm a little hard on her sometimes. It's just that I want her to be strong. And since I became strong on my own, I guess I think it's best if she becomes strong on her own, too.

But maybe I should revisit that.

I knock on her door. When I walk in, she politely mutes the TV. I can tell she's been crying.

"Listen," I say gently. "I know you hate having to sit at home because *I'm* not Susie High School."

"Like you care," she jibes. Her tone is

the one I usually use. Vintage Razorblade Sarcasm.

"I do care," I tell her. "But I'm a firm believer in doing something for your own reasons, not someone else's."

Bianca sighs. "I wish I had that luxury. I'm the only sophomore who got asked to the prom and I can't go, because *you* don't feel like it."

If only such things didn't matter to her.

But I guess they do.

It's time to tell her something real.

"Joey never told you we went out, did he?" I ask.

"Yeah . . . okay . . ." But I can tell Bianca has no idea.

"In ninth," I tell her. "For a month."

"Why?"

I can't help a little self-mockery. "He was, like, a total babe," I say in my best Valley Girl accent. Such things actually mattered to me then.

"But you *hate* Joey," Bianca says, still confused.

"Now I do."

"What happened?" she asks.

139

My expression must be really easy to read. I don't need to say a word. She gets it.

"No way," she says.

I can't believe I'm telling her this. But if I want her to start living by the truth, I can't exactly avoid it.

"Just once," I explain. "Right after Mom left. He seemed so understanding. Anyway, everyone was doing it, so I did it. Afterwards, I told him I didn't want to anymore. I wasn't ready. He got pissed. He dumped me. After that, I swore I'd never do anything just because everyone else was doing it. And I haven't since. Except for Bogey's party, and my stunning digestive pyrotechnics."

I was such a fool. I really believed that Joey and everything he represented could make me happy. I thought they could take the pain away. But they only made it worse.

Bianca is stunned. "How is it possible that I did not know this?" she asks.

I tell her I warned Joey that if he told anyone, the cheerleading squad would find out how . . . um . . . *tiny* he is.

"Okay." Bianca gets it. "But why didn't *you* tell me?"

140

"I wanted to let you make up your own mind about him," I answer. I don't even know if that's true. I hope it is.

"Then why did you help Daddy hold me hostage?" Bianca continues. "It's not like I'm stupid enough to repeat *your* mistakes."

But I didn't think I was stupid enough to make the mistakes in the first place. "I guess I thought I was protecting you," I say.

"By not letting me experience anything for myself?"

The question hangs in the air. It hurts because it's true. I can offer a hundred and one excuses. But they all contradict one another.

I pick up the strand of Mom's pearls from Bianca's nightstand.

"Not all experiences are good," I tell her. "You can't always trust the people you want to."

"I guess I'll never know, will I?" Bianca snaps back. She snatches the pearls out of my hand and throws them into the garbage. Then she leaves the room.

She is so angry. She is so sad.

Did I do this to her?

No. It wasn't all me.

But maybe it was partly me.

Early the next morning, I look out my window and see her sitting on our old tire swing. She could be four, or eight, or the fifteen she really is.

I feel so responsible.

When she gets back inside, I'm going to tell her I'm going to the prom.

47
Bianca

Only ten hours to prepare for the BIGGEST NIGHT OF MY LIFE! And without Daddy realizing it. Kat and I have agreed (was she touched by an angel?) the key to our plan is the element of surprise. It all has to be timed perfectly.

Daddy will never know what hit him.

We wait until Cameron's car pulls up. Then Kat zooms out the door, telling Daddy she's headed to the prom.

I follow quickly after, fully ready to go.

"What's that?" Daddy is stunned when I step into the living room. And it's not because I look stunning.

"A prom dress," I reply.

The doorbell rings. I run to open it (but not too fast, since I'm wearing heels). Cameron is waiting for me. He looks so much older in his tux. He looks so . . . *handsome*.

When he sees me, he's all, "Wow. I — you — Wow."

So sweet.

"Bye, Daddy!" I call. I kiss him on the cheek.

"Stop," he commands. "Turn. Explain."

This is the crucial moment.

I speak quickly: "Okay, remember how you said I could date if Kat dated? Well, she found this guy, who's actually kind of perfect for her, which is actually kind of perfect for me, because Cameron asked me to the prom and I really wanted to go, and now that Kat went, I'm allowed to — based on the above-mentioned rule and its previous stipulations, of course."

"Hold on," Daddy tries to protest.

But we're already out the door.

48
Kat

I cannot believe I am wearing a blue gown. I feel like such a *girl.*

Except when Patrick sees me.

Then I feel like a woman.

He's all dressed up, too, waiting for me in the ballroom lobby. I ask him how he got a tux at the last minute.

"Just something I had," he says casually. "You know. Lying around. Where'd you get the dress?"

"Just something I had," I reply. "You know. Lying around."

I can't stop looking at him.

He looks mighty fine.

I tell him I'm sorry I ever questioned his motives. I was so wrong.

I can't believe I'm at the prom.

"So," I say, "are you ready?"

He stares at me, taking me in.

"For you?" he asks. "Oh, yeah."

I blush as we walk inside.

Inside the ballroom, it's all . . . decorated. Like a Cinderella wonderland.

"Quite the ostentatious display," I observe. I don't want to succumb *entirely*.

I look around the room. Everyone seems so much older in their tuxes and gowns. And so much cleaner, too. It's like some trippy mix of *My So-Called Life* and *The X-Files*. Aliens have taken over my school and turned the students into attractive people.

Too too weird.

I see Cameron and Bianca dancing cheek-to-cheek and have to smile.

Good for her.

(I'm so glad it's not Joey.)

Mandella enters the hall nervously, wearing this long Elizabethan gown. If Shakespeare could only see her now — I swear, he'd never write another tragedy.

Yet I'm a little concerned, because it appears that Mandella thinks Big Will has asked her to the prom. But the truth ends up being even stranger. It's the head of the AV squad, Michael, dressed as the Bard.

Mandella's grin couldn't be wider.

She's in heaven.

The two of them head to the dance floor, and the two of us soon follow. Patrick and I have never danced before, but it doesn't take us long to find our rhythm. Of course, the band is pretty awful. Each slow song lasts about a million hours. Luckily, Patrick leans over to me and we start telling each other jokes. We can definitely make each other laugh.

We are having such a good time, despite the music. Then the strangest thing happens. The band starts its next song, and after the first three chords, I can tell my favorite band has taken the stage.

Impossible, I know.

But I look — and IT'S THEM!

Patrick smiles and says he called in a favor.

For me.

Wow.

49

Bianca

Kat is like a different person. As I'm walking to the ladies' room, I make eye contact with her, and I swear she's someone I haven't seen in years. Someone I used to get along with really well. Before everything happened.

The night is better than I could have possibly imagined. It's magic.

The ladies' room is totally full maintenance zone. I've just finished touching up my lipstick when Chastity walks in.

Chastity!?!

"What are you doing here?" I ask, surprised.

"Did you think you were the only sophomore at the prom?" she replies in a tone that makes me wonder why we were ever, ever, *ever* friends.

Then she tells me Joey just picked her up.

"Congratulations," I say. "He's all yours."

I *so* mean it.

"Very generous," Chastity responds cattily. Then she hits me with her best shot, snarling, "The only reason Joey went out with you was because he bet his friends he could *get with* you."

I am fuming. It takes all my restraint not to shove Chastity through the mirror.

But it's not really Chastity I'm mad at.

She's just stupid and deluded.

It's Joey who is the total scum.

50
Patrick

While we're slow-dancing, I confess to Kat, "Milwaukee."

At first she doesn't get it. So I explain, "That's where I was last year. I wasn't in jail. I don't know Marilyn Manson, and I've never been near a Spice Girl. My grandpa was sick, so I spent a year sitting on his couch, watching *Wheel of Fortune,* and making him SpaghettiOs. End of story."

Kat is delighted — and touched.

"No way," she says. But she knows I've given her the truth.

It's an almost perfect moment.

Then Joey comes up and ruins it all.

He's gone nuclear because Bianca came with Cameron, not him.

"I didn't *pay* you to take *Kat* out so that little punk could snake me with Bianca," he charges loudly.

The minute the words are out of his mouth, I know it's all over.

"Nothing in it for you, huh?" Kat rages. Then she storms off.

I follow her, hoping it's not too late.

51

Cameron

Michael sees what happens and decides it's time for us to act. I can't find Bianca, but perhaps that's for the best. Michael excuses himself from Mandella, and the two of us head for Joey.

"Joey, pal, compadre," Michael urges. "Let's take it easy."

Joey pushes Michael to the floor. I try to help him up.

"You messed with the wrong guy!" Joey yells. He is completely nutso. "You're going to pay. You and that witch."

Now *that's* totally uncalled for. "Okay, look, that's enough," I say, right at Joey. "Face it, the best man won."

Before I can do anything, I'm on the floor.

Joey just rails into me before I can defend myself. I'm about to get back up and fight when something astonishing happens.

There's a tap on Joey's shoulder. He turns and a fist smashes into his face.

Bianca's fist.

We're suddenly surrounded by Cowboys and Coffee Kids and White Rastas.

"That's for making my date bleed," Bianca says.

Joey's holding his nose. "I'm shooting a nose spray ad tomorrow!" he cries.

Bianca hits him again.

"That's for my sister," she says.

She hits him again.

"And that's for me."

I am amazed.

She is amazing.

Next, a Cowboy knocks Joey to the ground, yelling, "And that's for the fourth grade!"

Soon everyone is descending on Joey.

It's payback time.

I stand up. Bianca turns and kisses me.

"Are you okay?" she asks.

"I've never felt better."

And I mean that, with all my heart.

52
Kat

I cannot believe it. I am too angry and hurt and mortified for words.

It was all for money. Patrick was never into me. He never even liked me.

I am such a fool.

King Jerk Stalker Man Liar Creep has the *nerve* to follow me out of the ballroom.

I can't stand it.

"You were *paid* to take me out!" I shout at him. "By the one person I truly hate. I *knew* it was a setup."

"It wasn't like that," he pleads. As if he hasn't lied to me before.

"Really?" I say. "What *was* it like? A down payment now, then a bonus for sleeping with me?"

"I didn't care about the money. I cared about —"

I don't want to hear it.

"You are so not what I thought you were," I tell him. He grabs me and tries to kiss the problem away. But that won't work. Now I'm more sad than angry.

I've got to go.

I head straight back home and don't leave my room until the next morning. Then I head to the porch, to think for a while. Bianca comes out with a cup of tea, feeling sorry for me. She asks me if I want to come out sailing with her, Cameron, Mandella, and Michael. (Apparently, Mandella and Michael *really* hit it off at the prom.) She tells me it will be fun, but all I can muster in response is a vague, "I'm sure."

"I don't know if I thanked you for going last night," Bianca continues. "It meant a lot to me."

I tell her I'm glad. And really, I am. For her.

Then Cameron arrives, and Bianca's off to somewhere fun. I'm left on the porch. My father comes out to join me. He asks me if

Bianca left and I say, yeah, she's off with some bikers.

"Funny," Dad says, sitting on the railing, getting into his Heavy Bonding posture. Which is exactly what I don't need right now.

"So tell me about this dance," he goes on. "Was it hoppin'?"

"Parts of it," I reply.

"Which parts?" he asks.

"The part where Bianca beat the hell out of some guy," I report.

Dad is stunned. "Bianca did *what?*" he gasps.

"What's the matter?" I say. "Upset that I rubbed off on her?"

"No — impressed."

Wha —? Really? I'm stunned. I guess Dad notices, because he continues and says, "You know, fathers don't like to admit that their daughters are capable of running their own lives. It means we've become spectators. Bianca still lets me play a few innings. You've had me on the bench for years. When you go to Sarah Lawrence, I won't even be able to watch the game."

"*When* I go?" I repeat. If he lets me go to

156

Sarah Lawrence, I'll even forgive his convoluted sports metaphors.

"Don't tell me you've already changed your mind," he says. "I already sent them a check."

Goddess, sometimes people can surprise you. The person who never says anything right suddenly says everything right, and suddenly that's all that matters.

I give Dad a hug.

It's the least I can do.

53

Cameron

I am so happy, and at the same time I feel really guilty. Because Bianca and I are having this amazing time. And Michael and Mandella are having this amazing time. But Patrick and Kat are both miserable, and it's all because of the stupid money thing.

When I see Kat in the cafeteria on Monday, I go up to her and apologize.

"Kat," I say, "I'm really sorry."

She gives me this totally confused look and asks, "For what?"

"For everything that happened," I explain. "When Bianca asked me to find you a boyfriend, I had no idea it would turn out so —"

I don't get a chance to finish. A kill-kill-kill look flashes in Kat's eyes and she storms off.

What have I done now?

54
Kat

How dare she?

Betrayed by my own sister!

I storm into Bianca's English class and pull her out, claiming family emergency. In the hallway, Bianca tells me to let go. But there's no way she's getting off that easy.

"How could you set me up like that?" I yell.

"I just wanted —" she sputters.

"To completely damage me? To send me to therapy forever? What?"

"No! I just wanted —"

But before I can hear her bogus answer, Ms. Perky's shown up. She drags us to the guidance office and I explain the whole situation.

"So *you're* the real shrew," she says to Bianca. (Sometimes I think Ms. Perky's the one who needs the guidance and the counseling — I don't think she's got the whole adult thing down yet.)

To my surprise, Bianca says, "Yes! Okay! Yes — I'm the real shrew. I wanted her to get a boyfriend, so I could. Apparently, this makes me a horrible person. I'm sorry."

Then she turns to me and continues.

"I swear — I didn't know about the money. I didn't even know Joey was involved. I would never intentionally hurt you, Kat."

I don't want to believe it — but I do.

She's being sincere.

She's telling the truth.

It's hard to be angry after that.

She still owes me big time. But, moment of truth: I guess I owe her big time, too, for pretty much standing in the way of her life.

So I guess we'll consider it even.

Now I have to head to English class. I am dreading it. Not because of Mr. Morgan, but because of Patrick. He'll be there. I know it. And even though I've been thinking about him all weekend, I haven't actually seen him yet.

I'm really not sure what will happen when I do.

Of course, Joey is also in the class, and I'm really happy to see him — or, to be more specific, I'm really happy to see the miserable state he's in. He escaped the prom with two wicked black eyes and a shredded reputation. Even Mr. Morgan has a hard time hiding his pleasure.

Our homework assignment was to write a poem. I spent way too much time working on mine. I'd write it down, rip it up, then write it down again. When Mr. Morgan asks if there are any volunteers to read their poems aloud, I surprise myself by standing up. Patrick doesn't even look at me. But I don't care. I just have to say this. And whatever happens will happen.

It goes like this:

> *I hate the way you talk to me*
> *and the way you cut your hair.*
> *I hate the way you drive my car.*
> *I hate it when you stare.*
> *I hate your big dumb combat boots*
> *and the way you read my mind.*

*I hate you so much it makes me
    sick.
It even makes me rhyme.*

I take a breath and steal a quick look at
Patrick, who's staring at the floor. I don't
care. I continue.

*I hate the way you're always right.
I hate it when you lie.
I hate it when you make me laugh —
Even worse when you make me cry.
I hate it when you're not around
and the fact you didn't call.
But mostly I hate the way I don't
    hate you,
Not even close, not even a little bit,
Not even any at all.*

Now I look directly at Patrick. He looks
back this time.
    He knows. And I know he knows.
    I walk out of the room.
    Whatever happens will happen.

55

Cameron

I never thought happy endings could happen to a guy like me. I've been to so many schools, and have seen so many scenes, that I always assumed I would have to be satisfied with good and would never really see wonderful.

Bianca changes all that.

We have something special, and I want to do something special for her. I sneak her out of class and set up a romantic table for two on the empty soccer field. A corner of the world, just for us.

After I tell her to open her eyes, she says, "Oh, my God, Cameron."

That's all I need to hear.

"Now aren't you glad to skip algebra?" I ask. Then I add, because it's so apparent, "You're beautiful."

"Oh, really?" Bianca replies. "Then why haven't you even noticed I changed the part in my hair?"

I tell her I *did* notice. I just don't care.

"Thanks a lot!" she says.

"No," I start to explain, "it's just that I always knew there was more to you than what everyone else saw."

"What are you talking about?"

"The real you," I say. "You know, thoughts, feelings, your fears. I mean, you have some, right?"

She leans closer to me and says, "Like my fear of pastels."

Not exactly what I'd been thinking.

"Kidding," she says, and her smile lights up the world. "I'm really only afraid of plaids."

With that, we kiss.

It's a happy ending.

56
Kat

I head straight to my car. I've made my peace. Now I'm outta here.

I open the door and find a Fender Strato-caster and an amp reclining in the front seat.

I can't believe it.

I really can't believe it.

For once in my life, I'm speechless.

I spin around, and Patrick's right there.

My Lover Crooner Fairy Godmother Man. "Nice, huh?" he says.

"A Fender Strat," I say. "You bought this?"

How did he know?

"I thought you could use it," he tells me, real offhand. "You know, when you start your band."

I don't answer. I can barely hide my smile.

He steps closer.

"Besides," he continues, "I had some extra cash. Some jerk paid me to take out this really great girl."

"Is that right?"

"Yeah, but then I screwed things up. I fell for her."

I can't look him in the eyes. I'll give everything away.

"Really . . ." I murmur.

How did he find out?

"It's not every day you find a girl who'll distract a teacher to get you out of detention," he croons.

I'm embarrassed and flustered and happy. I lift my head and he kisses me.

And I let him.

For a moment.

Then I break it off.

I want to make one thing perfectly clear to him.

"You can't just buy me a guitar every time you mess up, you know," I say.

"I know," he agrees. "But there's still

drums and a bass, and maybe even some-day a tambourine."

He kisses me again.

Again, I break it off.

"And don't just think you can —"

This time he kisses me and I don't want to end it. I kiss him back, and that's where we are. He hasn't tamed me, but he's made me happy. I haven't tamed him, but I'm with him all the same.

End of story.

Roll credits.

One Last Word From Mandella

I would just like to tell you that the story you just read is loosely based on a play by the man who is, in my humble opinion, the most brilliant, fascinating playwright and poet who ever lived: William Shakespeare.

The name of the play is *The Taming of the Shrew.* It is about a headstrong woman named Katharina (they didn't call people Kat in those days) and her fair sister, Bianca. They live in the town of Padua, with their father, Baptista. He has a rule that Bianca, who is loved by many, cannot marry until Kat, who is loved by none, marries. Bianca doesn't take this well. Katharina couldn't care less.

Then along come the men. Lucentio, like

Cameron in our story, sees Bianca and at once falls madly in love. With the help of his servant Tranio, Lucentio manages to get rid of Bianca's other King Jerk suitor, Hortensio, and make himself known to Bianca. There's only one hitch — in order to marry Bianca, Katharina must wed first.

Enter Petruchio from Verona. (That's Patrick Verona to you.) He is as headstrong as Katharina . . . and becomes determined to make her his wife. At first, it's a game to him. But then he — and Katharina — fall in love. It takes all their strength to admit it to themselves. But eventually they get through to each other.

Of course, Shakespeare says this all much, much better than I can. So you should really go and read *The Taming of the Shrew.*

Really.

Do it.

Now.